U0546156

尪仔衫
蘇善雙語囝仔詩

Puppet Suits: Suzanne's Bilingual Poetry for Children

圖・文／蘇 善

頭前詩
Introducing Lyrics

囡仔時

逐項奇

四季攏趣味

In every childhood

All looks extraordinary

Seasons collect things fine and good

目次
Contents

頭前詩 Introducing Lyrics　　3

01　蝶仔花　Butterfly Ginger　　7
02　放風吹　Fly the Kite　　9
03　弓蕉園　Banana Field　　11
04　吊燈仔　Little Pendant　　13
05　戲棚跤　Under the Platform　　15
06　巡田水　Patrol the Field　　17
07　黑狗兄　Brother Doggy Black　　19
08　日頭燃水　Sun Heat Bath　　21
09　露螺　Snails　　23
10　摸龍眼　Scoop Longans　　25
11　菜瓜棚　Luffa Grid　　27

目次
Contents

12　武車 Solider's Bicycle　29

13　晃鞦韆 Swing Joy　31

14　食涼 Ice Food　33

15　磅米芳 Pop Rice　35

16　炕窯 Earth Oven　37

17　尪仔衫 Puppet Suits　39

18　眠床 Bed Stage　41

19　水拹仔 Hand Pump　43

20　含笑 Beams　45

話尾 Ending Words　46

關於作者 About Author　47

蘇善‧詩集創作 Suzanne's Poetry Collection　48

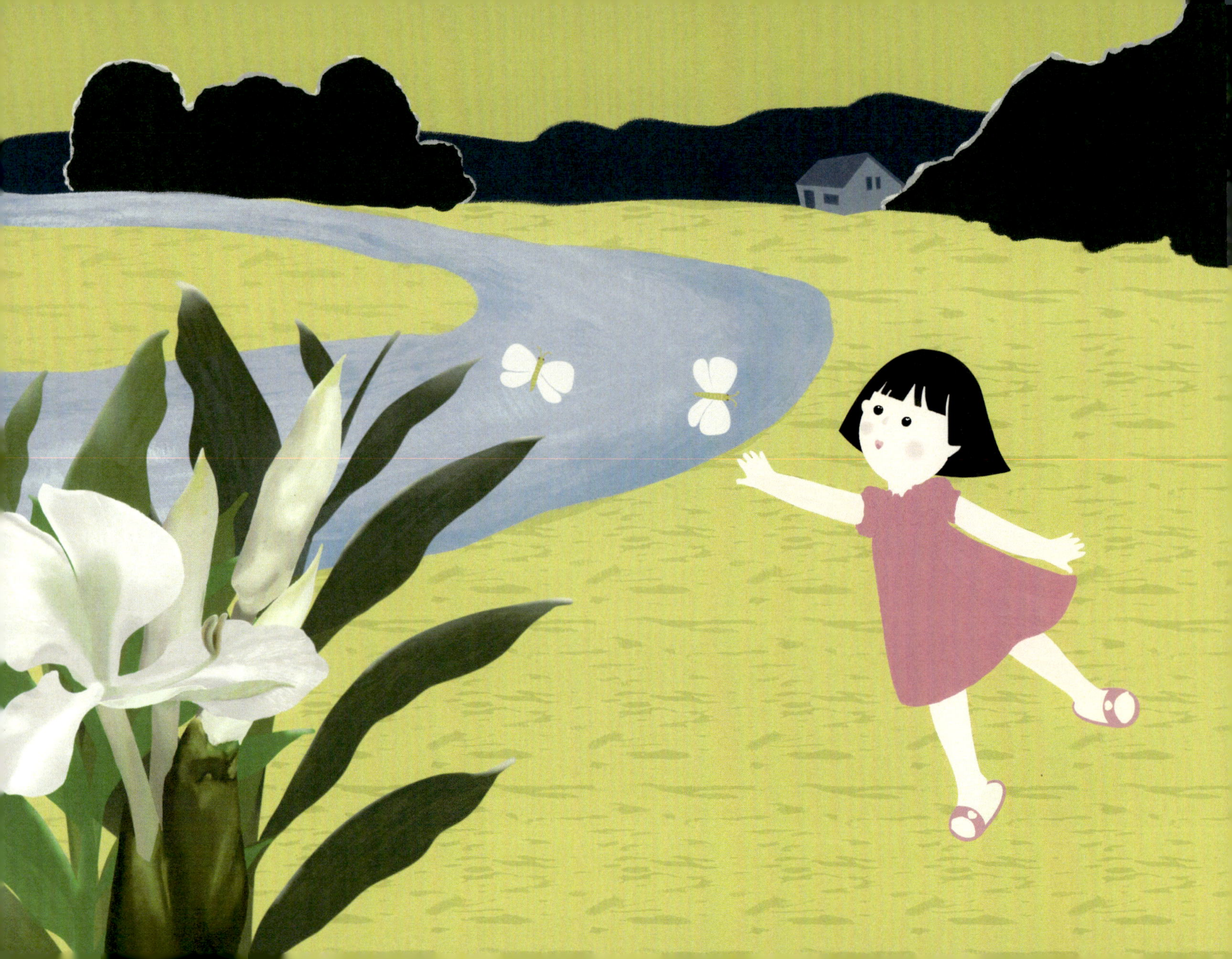

01 蝶仔花
Butterfly Ginger

蝶仔花	Butterfly ginger
想欲飛	Wishes to fly
飛過彼條溪	And fly across the stream.
彼條溪	That stream,
清清涼涼	Clear and cool,
種西瓜	Grows watermelons supreme.
（蝶仔花，飛呀飛）	(Butterfly ginger, fly and fly.)
蝶仔花	Butterfly ginger
想欲飛	Wishes to fly.
飛去揣阿妹	Then fly to visit my sister.
阮小妹	My little dear,
白白嬌嬌	Fair and pretty,
學講話	Learns from tongue twister.
（蝶仔花，飛呀飛）	(Butterfly ginger, fly and fly.)

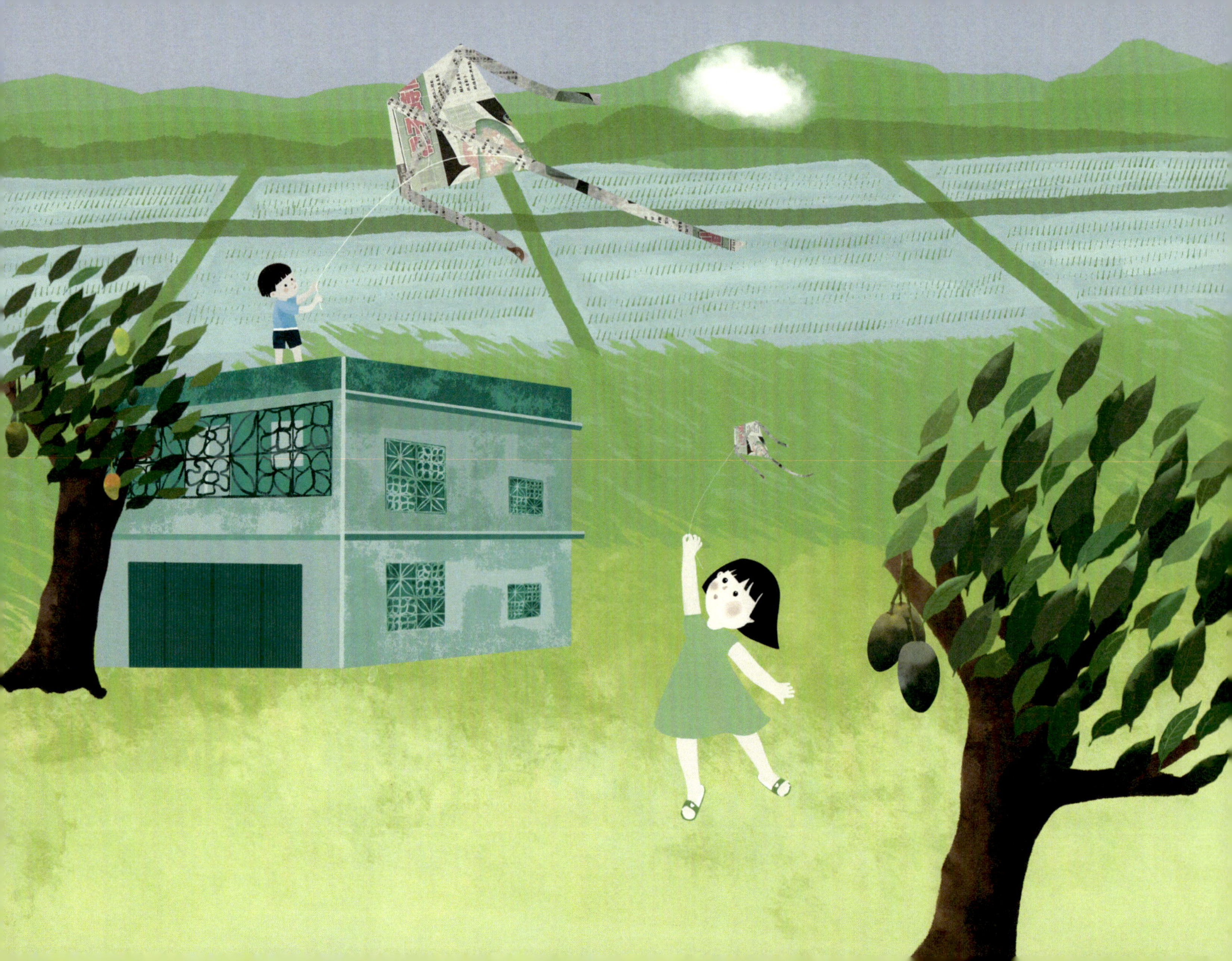

02 放風吹
Fly the Kite

啥人放風吹	Who is flying kites,
放去山邊	To the mountain,
放去溪邊	To the stream,
放去田邊	To the field,
做陣踅呀踅	All along riding joy?
一隻粉鳥仔四界飛	A pigeon also flies sound,
踅呀踅	Roaming around.
毋免走去樓頂	Don't climb to the rooftop.
毋免爬去樹仔尾	Don't climb to the treetop.
手舉懸	Just raise your hand light.
學快馬	Run as fast as a horse does.
戶埕踅呀踅	Gallop in the yard.
一粒黃樣仔滾落地	A yellow mango falls to the ground,
踅呀踅	Roaming around.

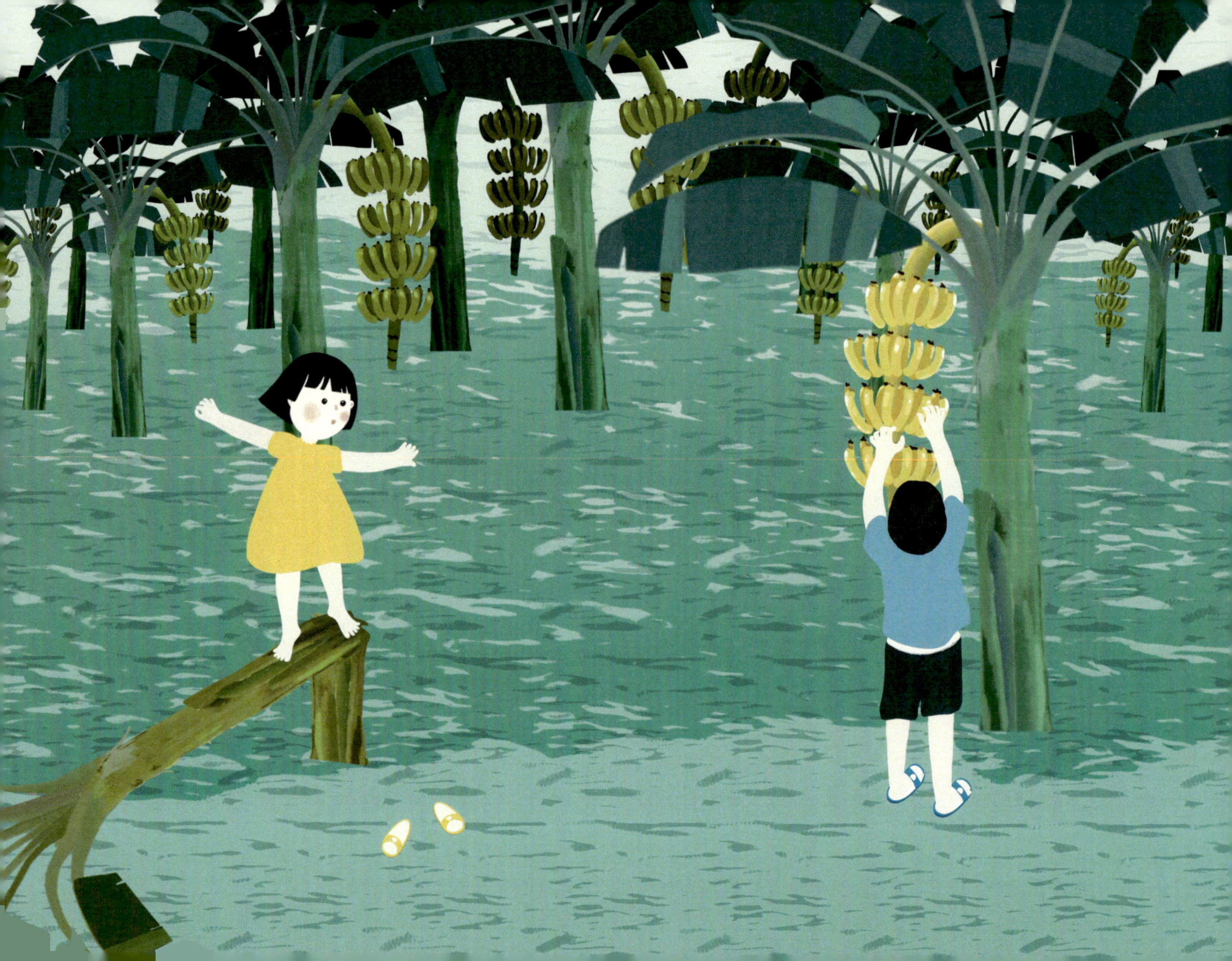

03 弓蕉園
Banana Field

弓蕉園	In Banana field,
弓蕉黃	Bananas grow ripe in yellow.
一條做早頓	One for breakfast,
一條留予明仔載	One is left for tomorrow.
巡田的白翎鷥	Little egret patrols
替阮阿伯	For my uncle,
趕走粟鳥仔群	Driving away the flock of sparrow.
弓蕉園	Banana field comes to hail.
遊樂園	What a place of amusement.
有人走頭前	One runs for head start.
有人拚命藏尾溜	One tries to hide the tail.
金爍爍的目睭	With eyes glittering,
兩步三步	In a second or two,
揣著家己的岫	Each invents his nest of heart.

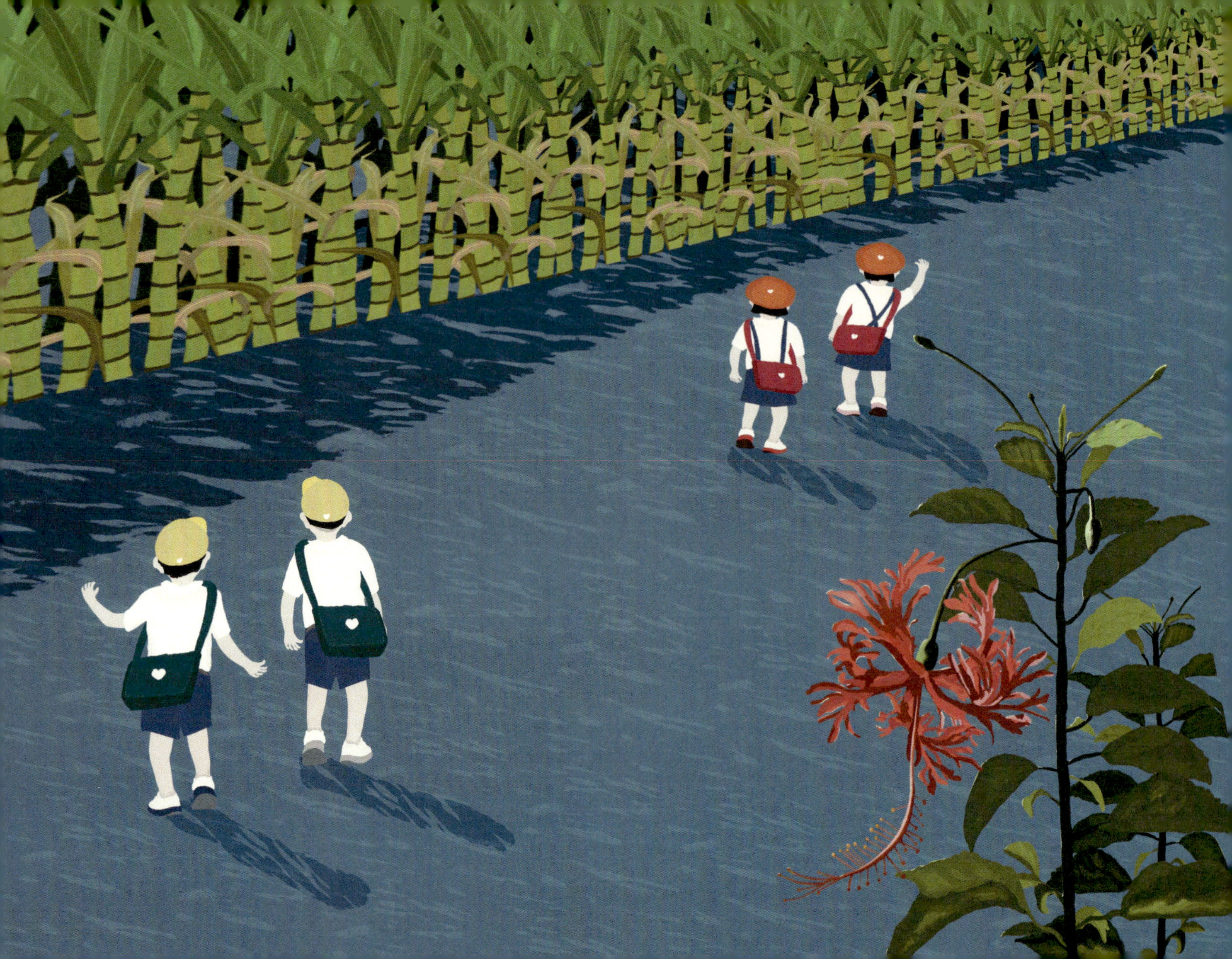

04 吊燈仔
Little Pendant

讀冊的路 On the way to school

做陣行 Carefully we patrol.

互相借膽 Boost our courage one another.

甘蔗葉仔橫霸霸 Sugarcane leaves look dreadful.

恬恬有風聲 Quiet rumor has it

毋知匿啥 That something hidden

害人生驚 Shall come out with a shock.

轉來的路 On the back way home

吊燈仔 Little pendant awaits

暗暝借光 Sharing glints with the night.

一葩電火紅絳絳 Its light ball shines reddish fire.

恬恬有笑聲 Quiet laugh has it

熱心攑手 That hands waving

問人枵飽 Shall salute with a feast.

乾興閣

05 戲棚跤
Under the Platform

大廟邊	Beside the temple
懸戲棚	Stands a huge platform.
鑼鼓拍起	Gongs and drums are beating,
布袋尪仔欲出戲	While glove puppets show up
扮仙謝神	Playing gods for appreciation,
搖搖擺擺	And with a waddle,
行踏黑白的武林	Stepping in the fictional world.
戲棚跤	Under the platform
揣曠闊	Sits a vast dwelling
坐落時間	Wherein time resides.
大人囡仔金金看	Young and old all fix a look
文生武生愛唸詩	On the puppets' chanting.
掌中搬弄世界	By manipulating world in hands,
啥人阿爸遮爾厲害	Whose dad is the master of retelling?

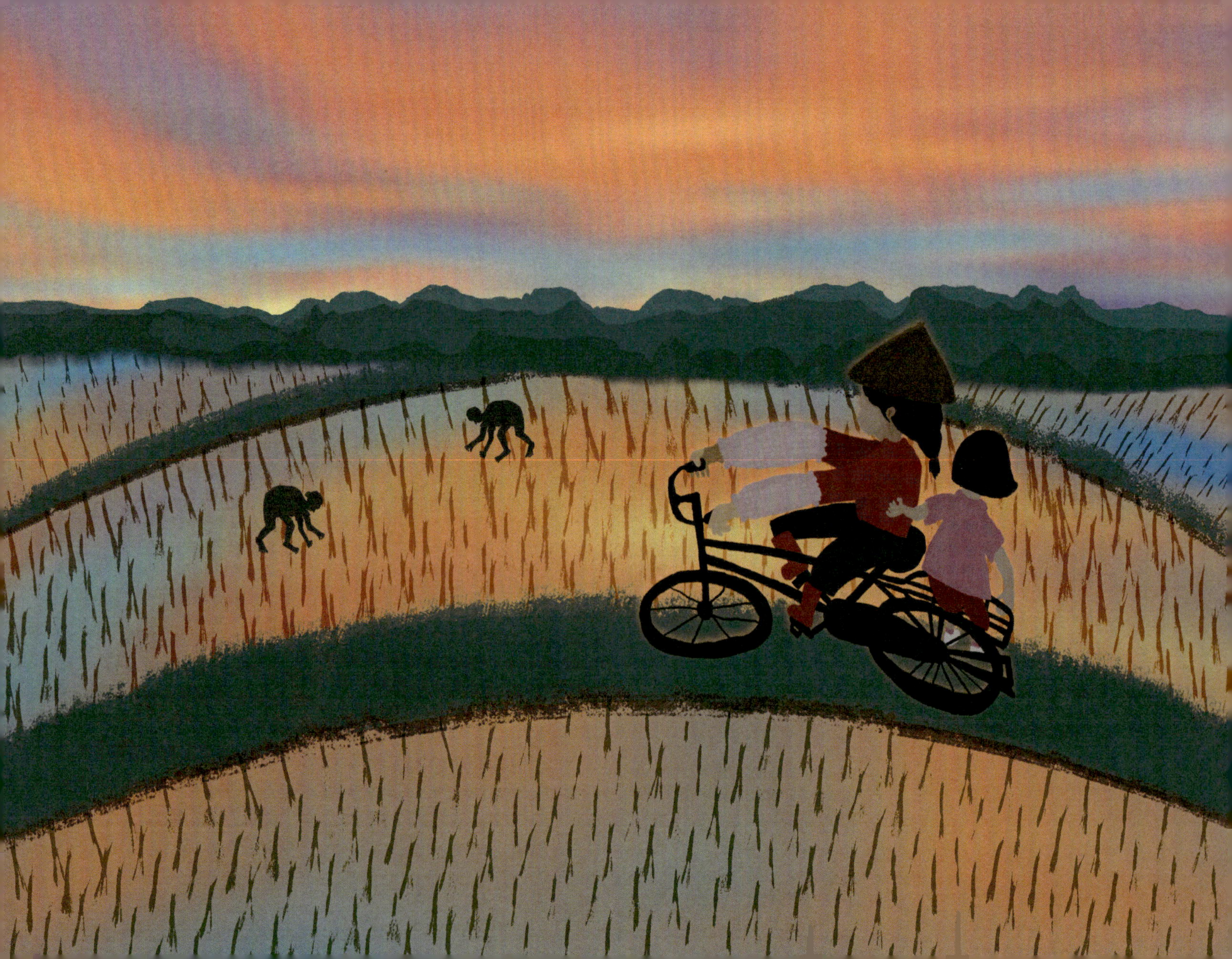

06　巡田水
Patrol the Field

天未光	Before day lights,
巡田園	Take a patrol in the field.
目睭毋願展	Yet eyes hold the lids
黏黐黐	Stickily.
武車後斗若搖椅	The backseat of bike jiggles
晃過頭	So heavily
一个夢斷線絲	That a dream along tears.
烏暗時	In the dark morning,
巡田水	Take a patrol in the field.
跤手愛細膩	Move with cares
沓沓仔行	Leisurely.
緊挲草	Speed up the weeding.
爛塗清氣	Keep the dirt clean and fresh.
一區稻仔笑瞇瞇	The rice shall grow giggles.

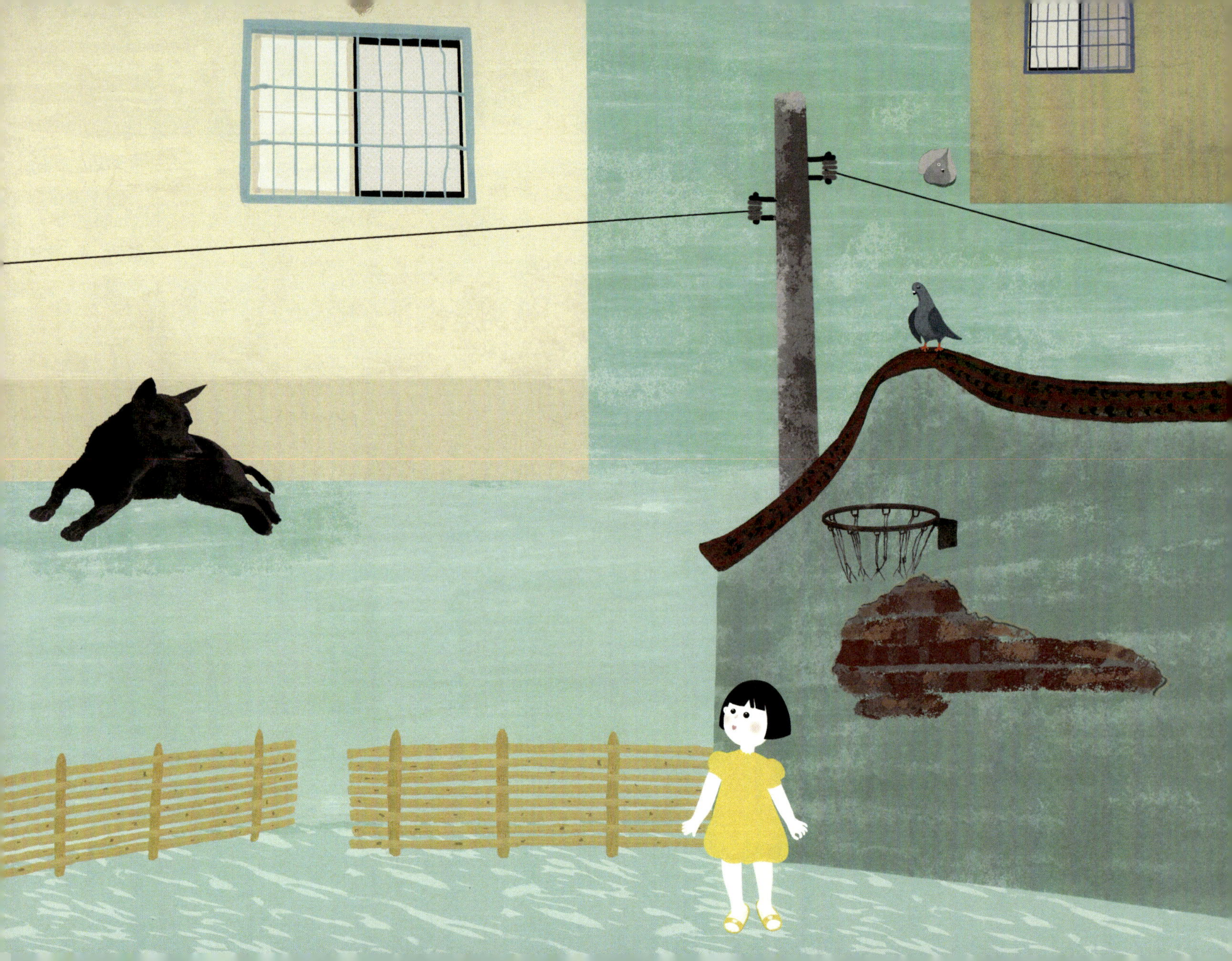

07 黑狗兄
Brother Doggy Black

黑狗兄	Brother Doggy Black
愛顧壁	Prefers lying by the wall.
後壁的後壁	In the back of the rear wall
一條路無人行踏	Stretches a road without stroller.
粉鳥仔兩三隻	Few pigeons there linger.
一隻盹龜	One is taking a nap,
一隻趴定定	One settles itself in a lap.
一隻飛過電火柱仔	One flies over the utility pole
揣樹影	For the shadows of trees.
一隻歇去別人的門口埕	One perches upon the next yard,
等半晡	Waiting all the afternoon
等無粟仔	Not getting any grain.
也等無半隻蟲	Not even a worm
暈暈佇塗跤	Falls into a swoon.

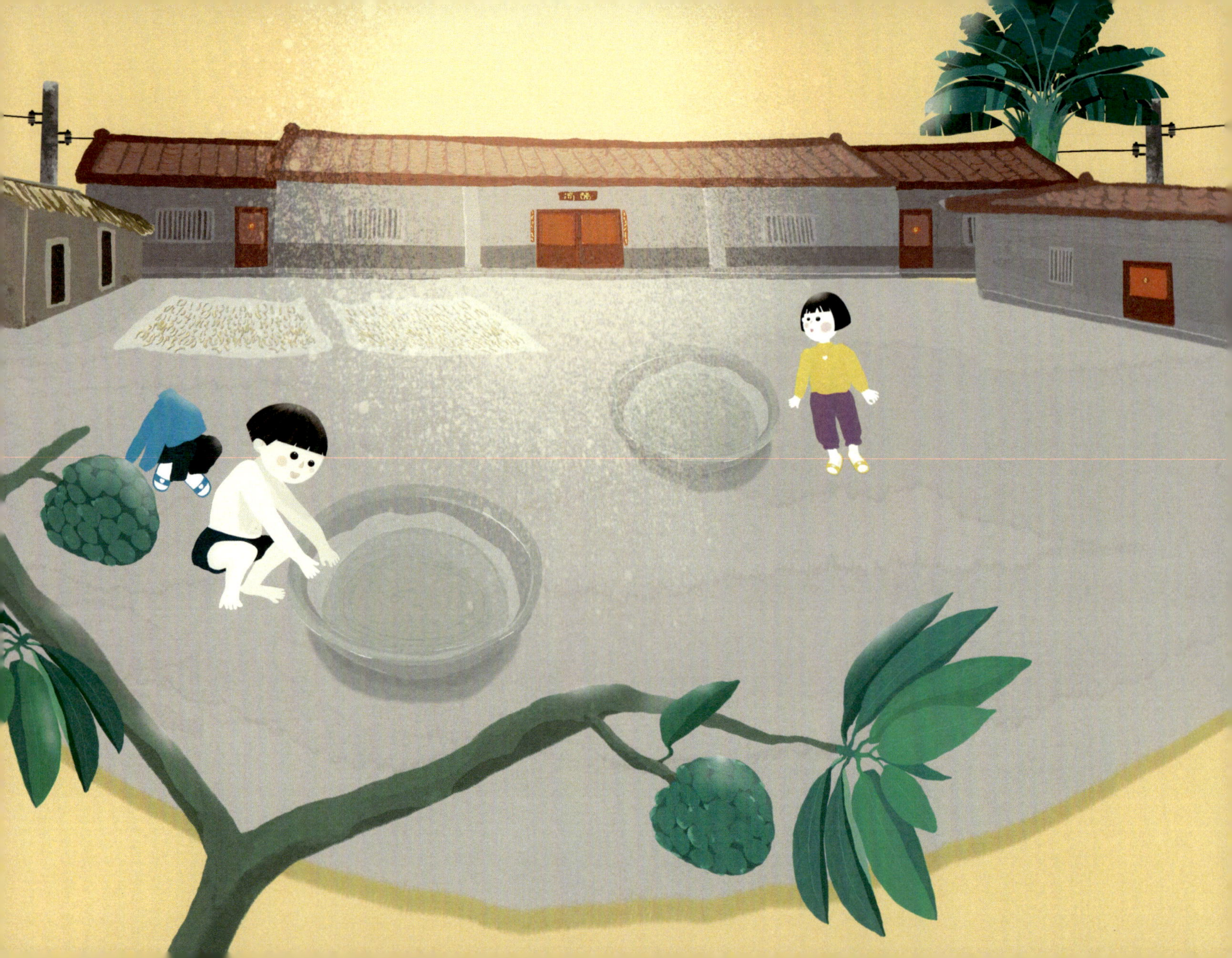

08 日頭燃水
Sun Heat Bath

大面桶	There big tin tub is
洗衫褲	Used to wash clothes.
小面桶	While the small one
定定收菜脯	Aims for collecting dried radishes.
攏總排來門口埕	All line up in the yard.
八分填	Water nearly filled up
欲等日頭燃燒水	Waits for sun boiling.
日頭燃水燒滾滾	Sun is heating the water.
毋驚冷風鑽	Ignore the chilly wind.
褪衫洗身軀	Go Undressing for a bath.
緊跤緊手	Do it in a hurry,
搶著大面桶	Grab the big tin tub.
小面桶	While the small one
留予睏晝的蟲	Shalll be left for a napping dub.

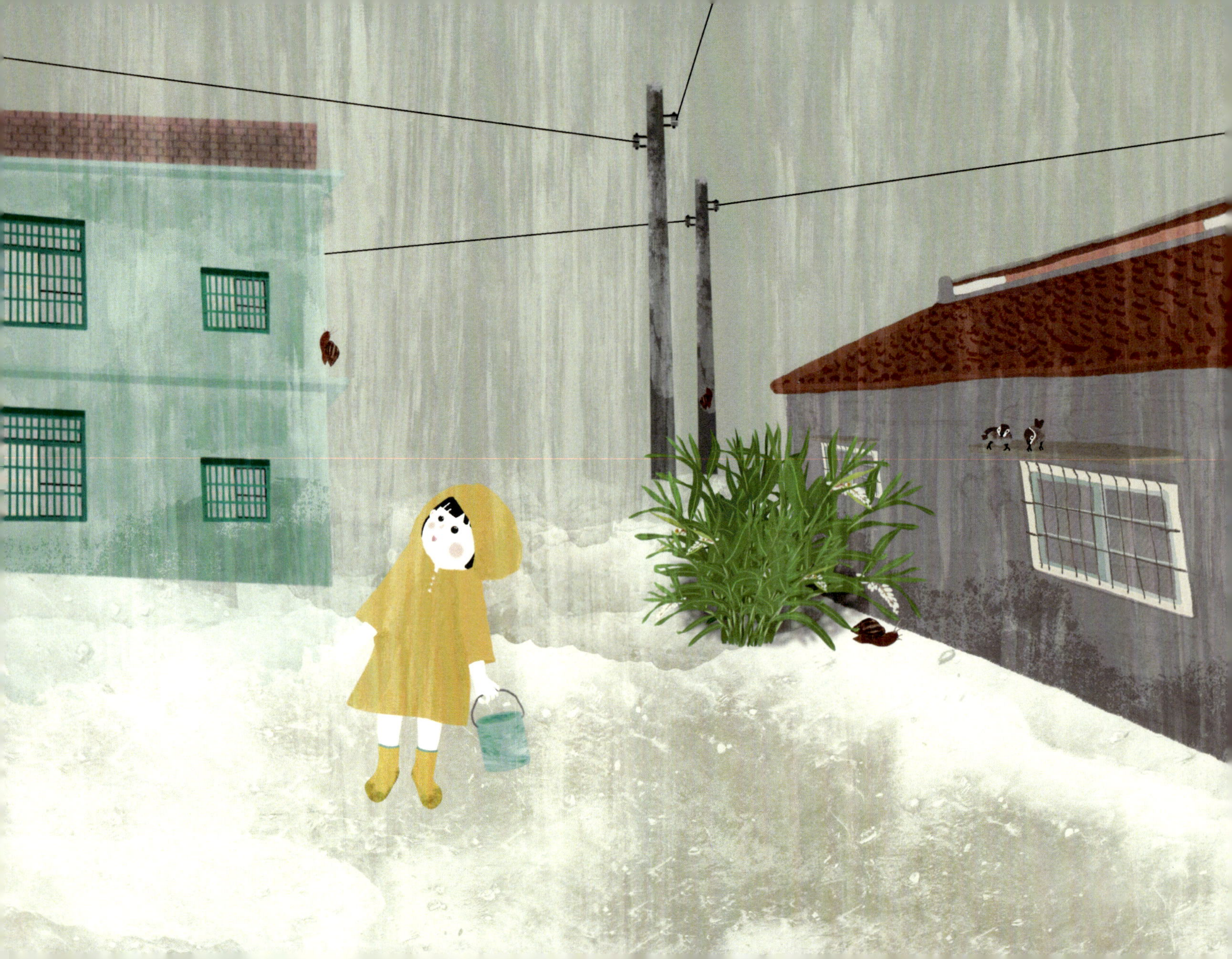

09 露螺
Snails

雨水厚	Heavy rain.
月桃恬恬開花	Shell ginger quietly blooms
顧厝後	While watching the back of house.
佗位來的露螺	Snails from nowhere
蟯蟯趖	Wander here and there.
是欲揣蟲	Do they go hunting bugs
抑是欲鼻芳	Or catching the perfumes?
佗位來的露螺	Snails form nowhere,
哪毋趕緊走	Why don't you go away?
戇戇踅	And stop the silly strolling.
這隻挲壁	This climbs over the wall.
彼隻攬著電火柱	That clings to the utility pole.
粟鳥仔搖頭	Sparrows shake their heads
想未曉	Not reading the play.

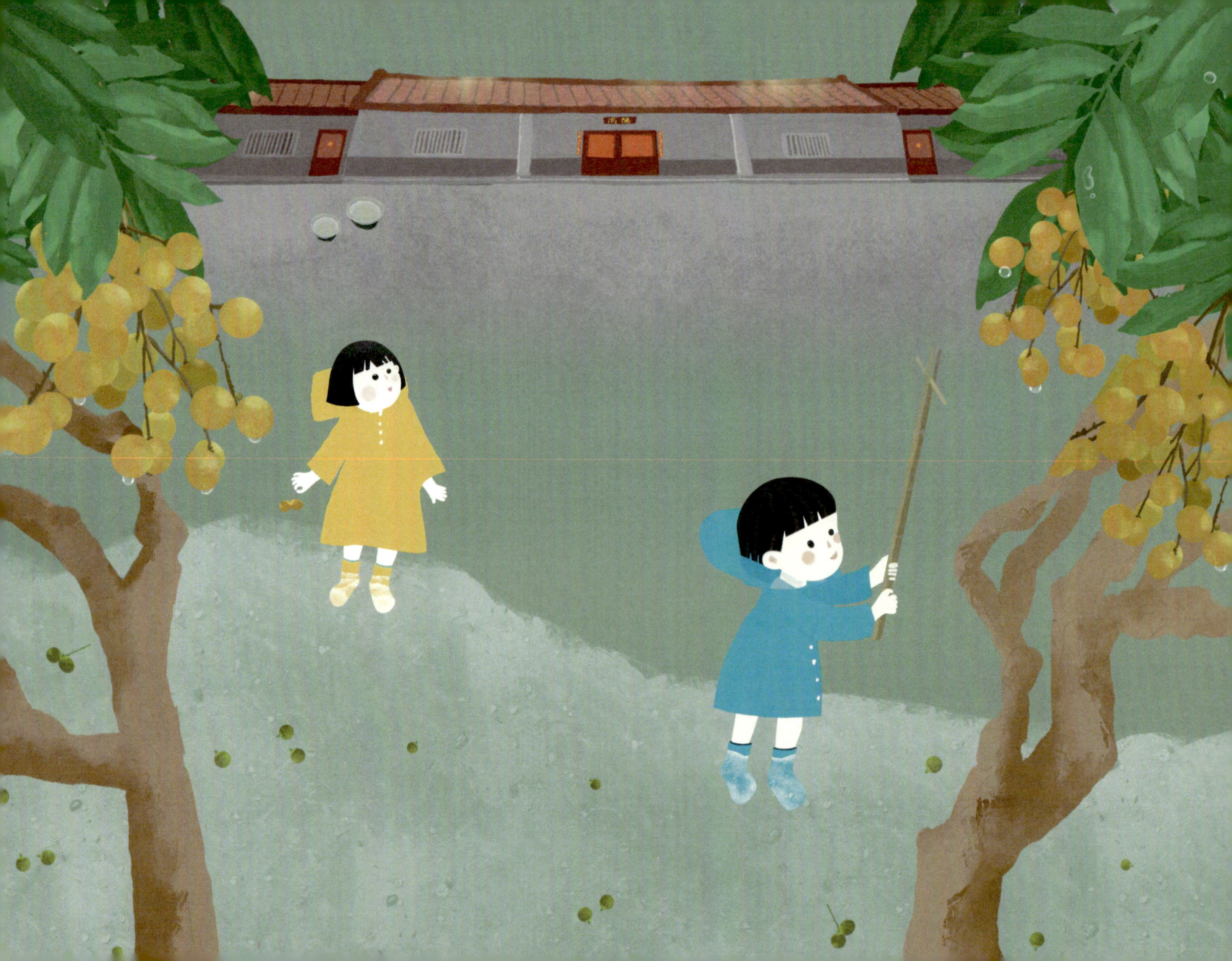

10 摸龍眼
Scoop Longans

風颱走   Typhoon goes away.
樹仔哮   Trees cry over big shower.
龍眼拍落若石頭   Longans are swept astray.
一粒一粒浸水   One and one soak in water,
驚殕又驚臭   In fear of getting rotted and sour.
誰人啊   Call for help.
緊來撈   Come and scoop all.

穿雨幔   Put on the raincoat.
緊來撈   Come and scoop all.
抾起龍眼像瑪瑙   Cherish longan like agate.
一粒一粒拭焦   One by one scrub as you could,
歇風又歇瀾   Letting it dry and scour.
哎喲喂   What dears!
敢好食   May it taste good.

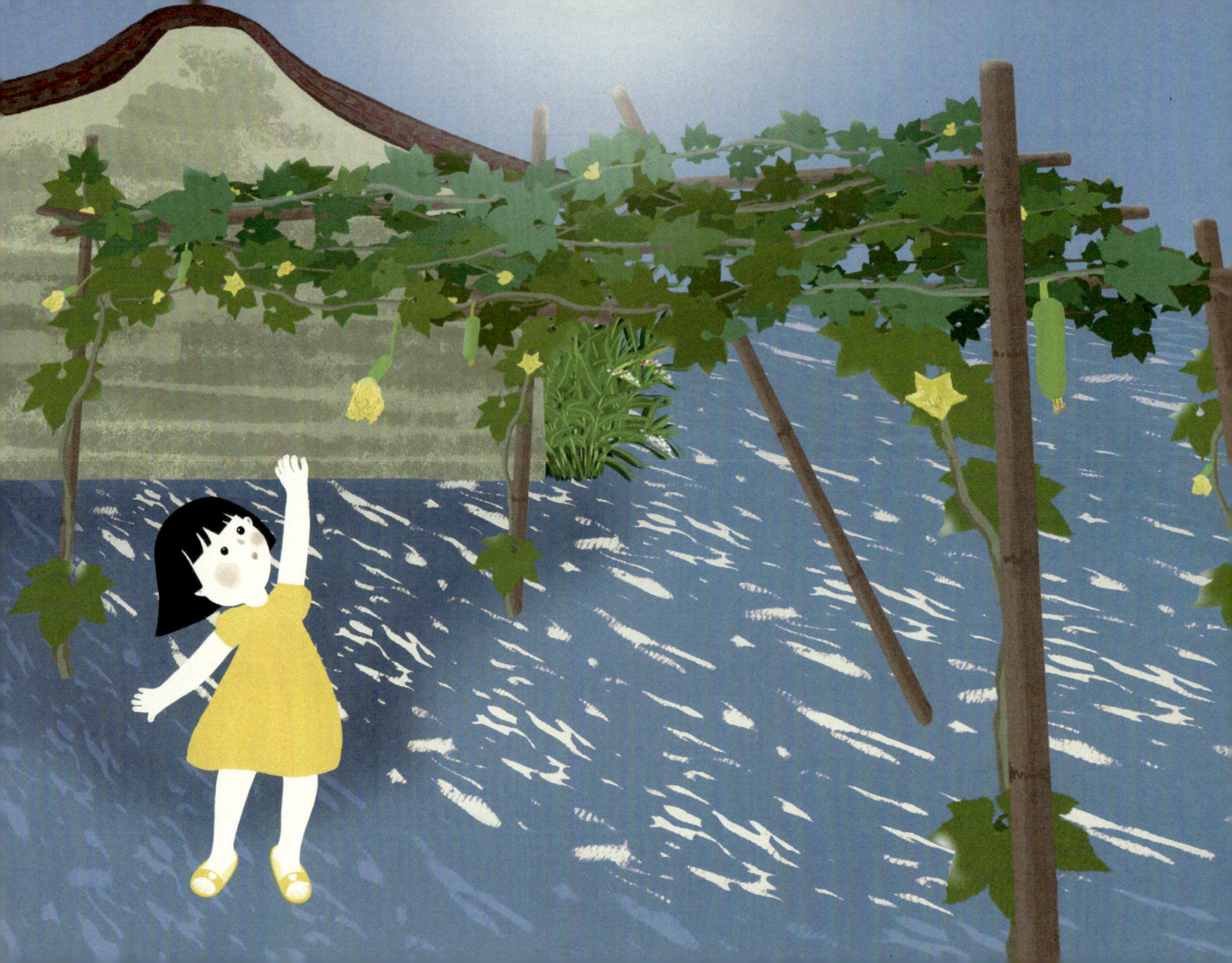

11 菜瓜棚
Luffa Grid

哪會遮爾嬌	What a pretty!
遮爾神奇	So amazingly
懸藤四界去	Crawling around the vines
開花滿滿是	Bloom in full flourish.
一蕊掛星	One drapes with stars,
一蕊掛月	And one hangs the moon,
毋驚凍露水	Regardless of chilling dew.
阿母的菜瓜棚	Where mom's luffa grid sits
遮爾趣味	There pleasures overflow.
懸藤走四季	Vines crawl over seasons,
險險焦蔫去	Nearly get dried out of nourish.
有蟲來喫	Insects come for bites.
有蜂鬥飼	Yet bees help grow
著時花又開	Into flower when time in due.

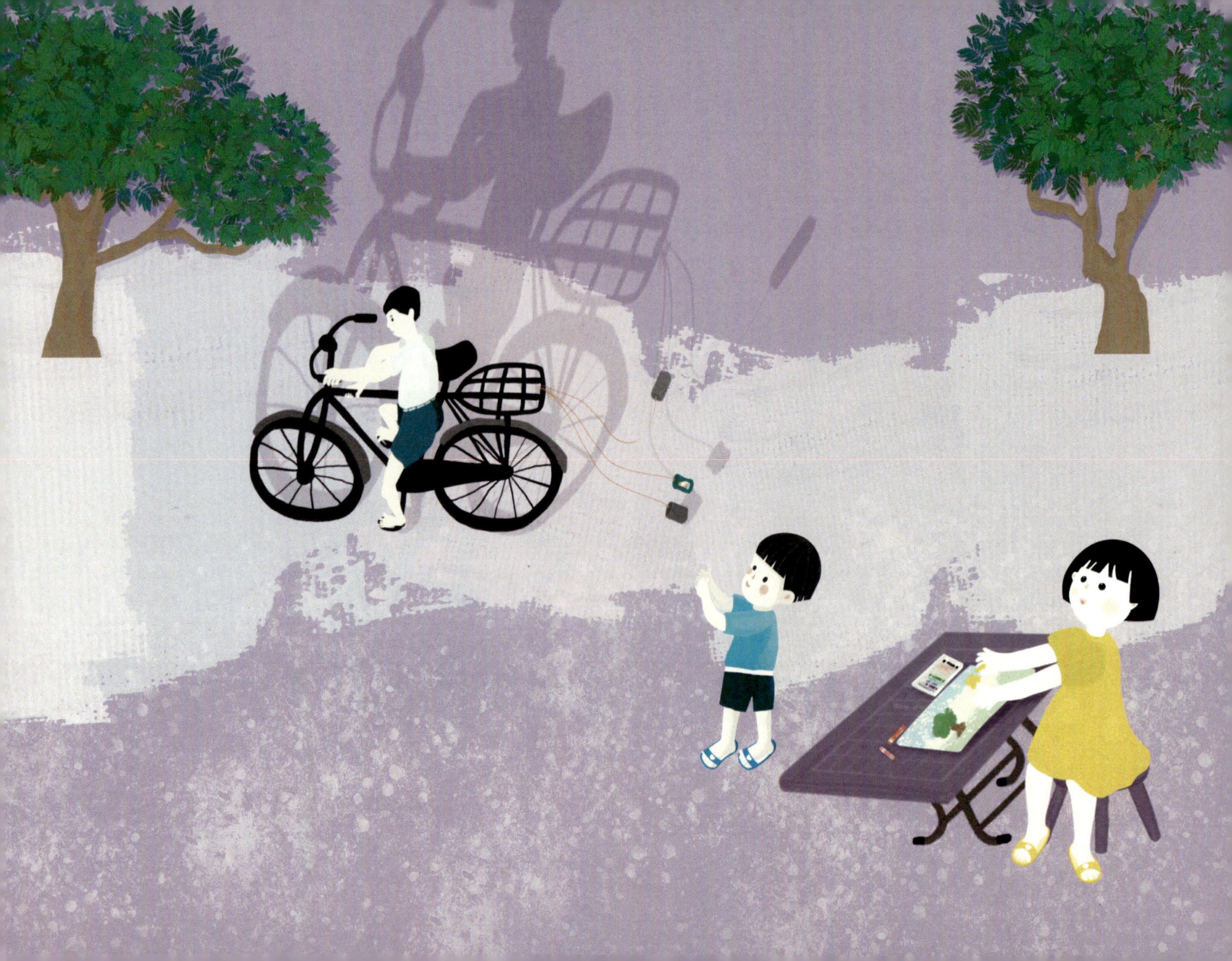

12 武車
Solider's Bicycle

大人的武車	That is a solider's bicycle
囂俳的烏影	Showing off it's shadow.
隔壁阿哥歪頭	The next door brother tilts head,
身軀若橫柴	And his body stiffs like a stick.
三个銅罐仔鬥喝聲	Three tin cans wildly jangle.
無人敢拍噗仔	Neither urges flare,
只好目睭金金看	Therefore I simply stare.
隔壁阿哥學踏車	The brother exercises in cycling,
一輪撞樹頭	Once hitting the tree head,
兩輪趴塗跤	Twice tumbling to the ground,
踅來踅去	Round and round.
三个銅罐仔鬥喝聲	Three tin cans wildly jangle.
粟鳥仔無愛看	Sparrows pass the guerre
飛上厝頂等月影	Flying upon the roof for clair.

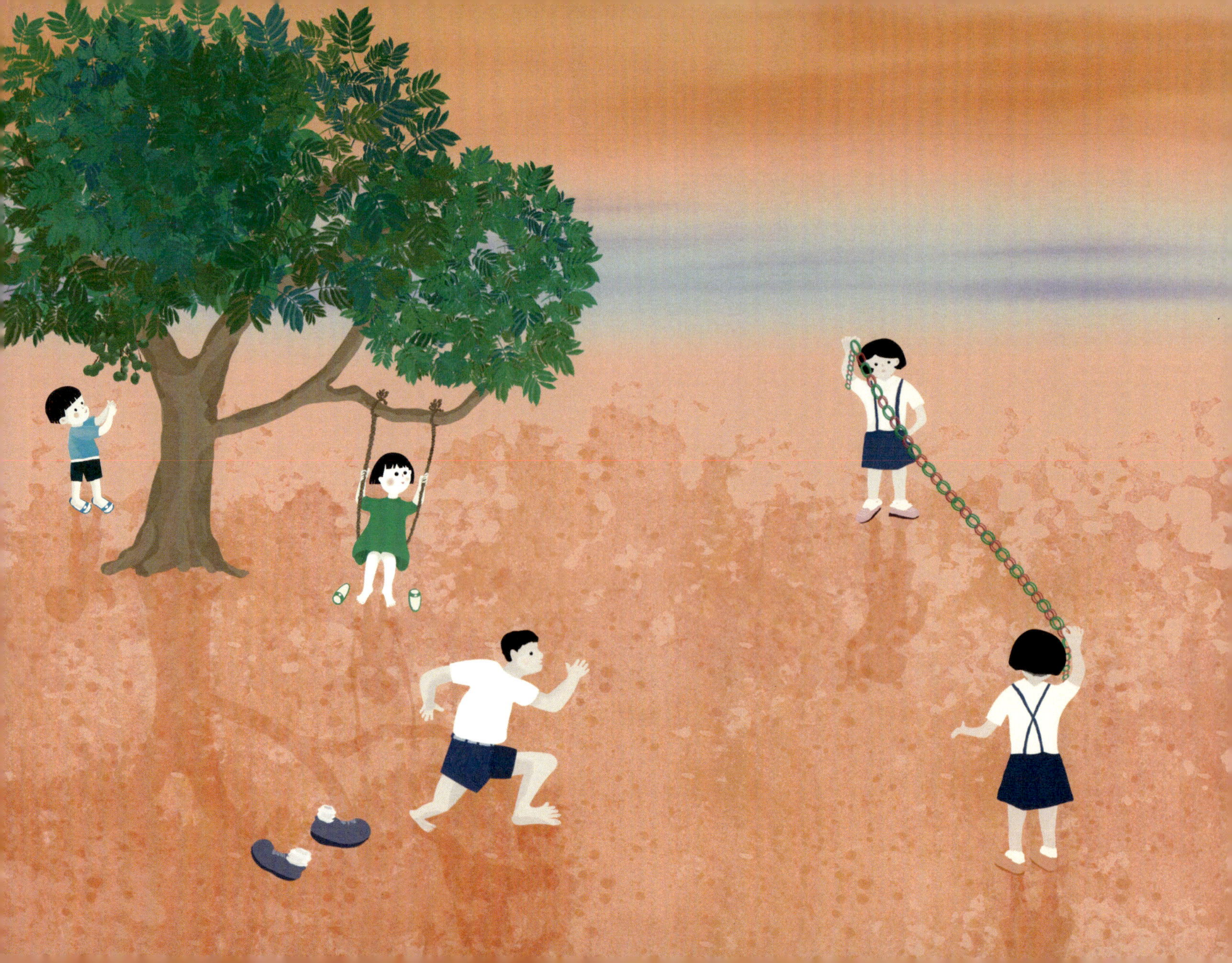

13 晃鞦韆
Swing Joy

下晡時	Late in the afternoon
日頭紅熾熾	The sun is setting red.
冊包仔放一邊	Put the school bag aside.
樹乳繩仔挲出來	Pull up the rubber band rope.
一坎一坎跳過	Jump higher and higher,
上懸的	Till the very top.
著愛用飛的	Flying seems best great.
下晡時	In the late afternoon
彩雲嬌噹噹	Clouds play color spread.
點心放一邊	Put the goodies aside.
稻草繩仔綁起來	Tie up the straw rope.
鞦韆歡喜振動	Swing joy and cheer.
欲耍心適的	Just for amusement,
勻勻仔晃	Slowness shall be straight.

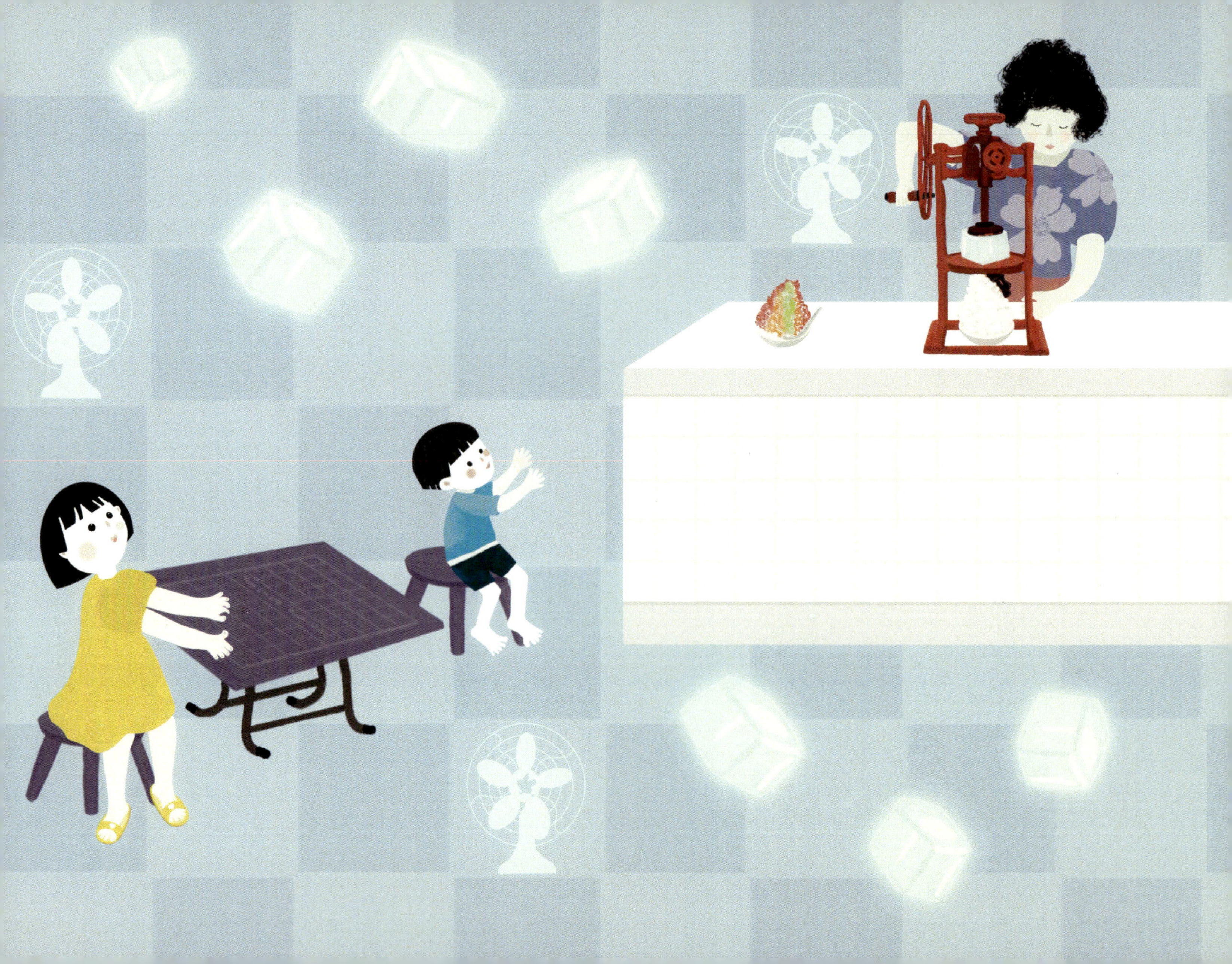

14 食涼
Ice Food

熱翕翕	Hot and choky,
覕無路	No way to get rid of the heat.
樹仔憂頭結面	Trees worry and sweat
等落雨	For rain drops.
電風強欲哮	Fans roar with tears.
吹暝吹日	After winding night and day
身軀定定一苞火	The body shall blast away.
燒燙燙	Burning hot
愛食涼	Makes need for ice food.
青草愛玉粉粿	Herb tea, Aiyu jelly and starch jelly,
紅豆綠豆仔木瓜簽	Azuki bean, mung bean and papaya shred.
啊，清冰上合意	Ah, shaved ice never fails to please.
淋糖水	Sprinkling with syrup,
炎天就冷吱吱	Summer heats instantly freeze.

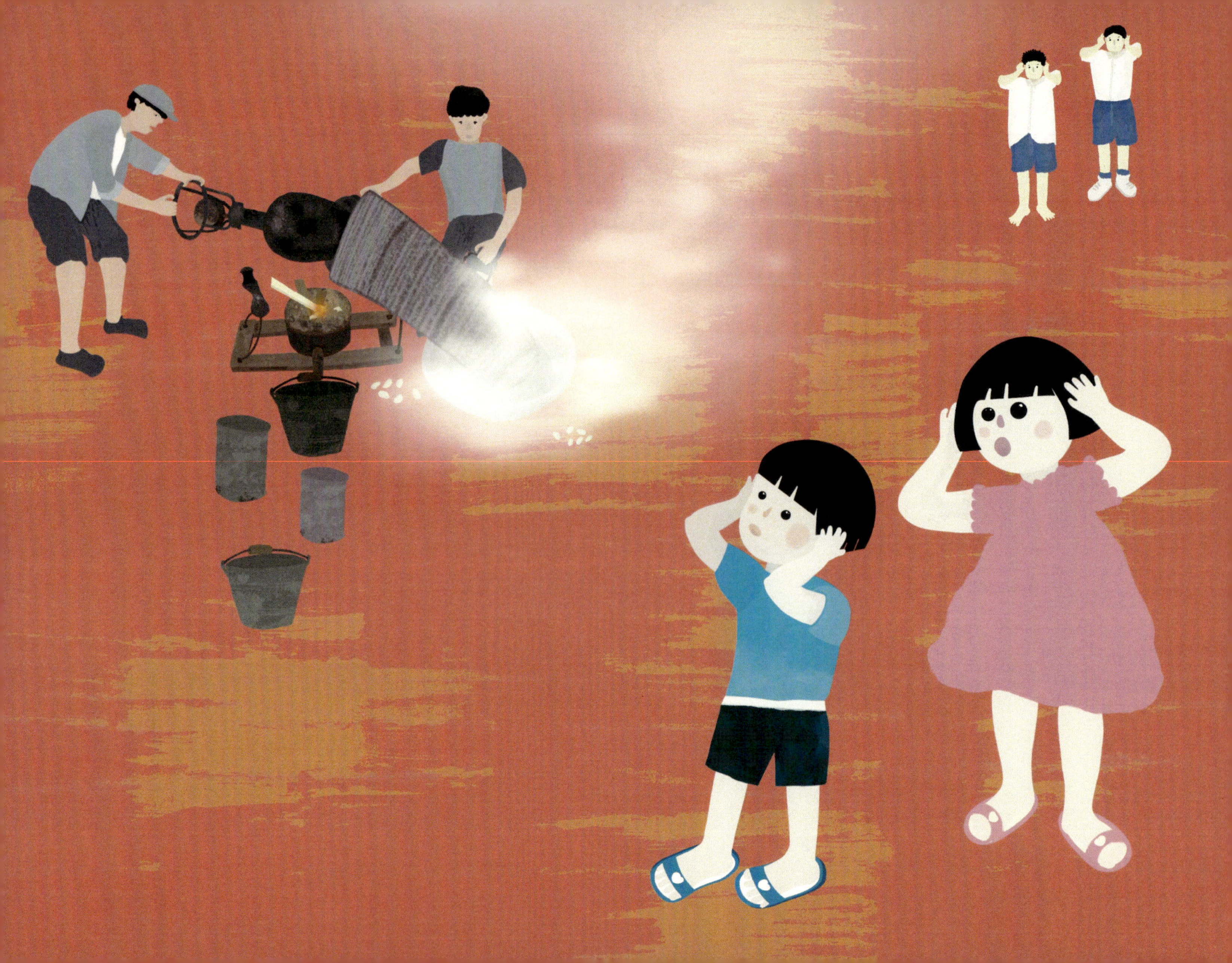

15 磅米芳
Pop Rice

磅米芳

掩耳孔

走去三里外

毋敢喘氣

目睭瞪大蕊

一陣煙

衝出臭火焦的芳味

磅米芳

世界振動

米粒仔彈到蟲

算伊好運抾著夢

白泡泡的夢

毋管囡仔抑大人

攏愛這款

Pop rice!

Cover all ears.

Run three miles away,

Never let your breath spray.

But keep eyes wide.

Behold a big smoke

Bursting out the scorching savor.

Pop rice!

Tremble all creatures.

Bouncing grains hit some worm.

What a luck to grab the dream,

White and crunchy.

Either young or old

Always love this unique flavor.

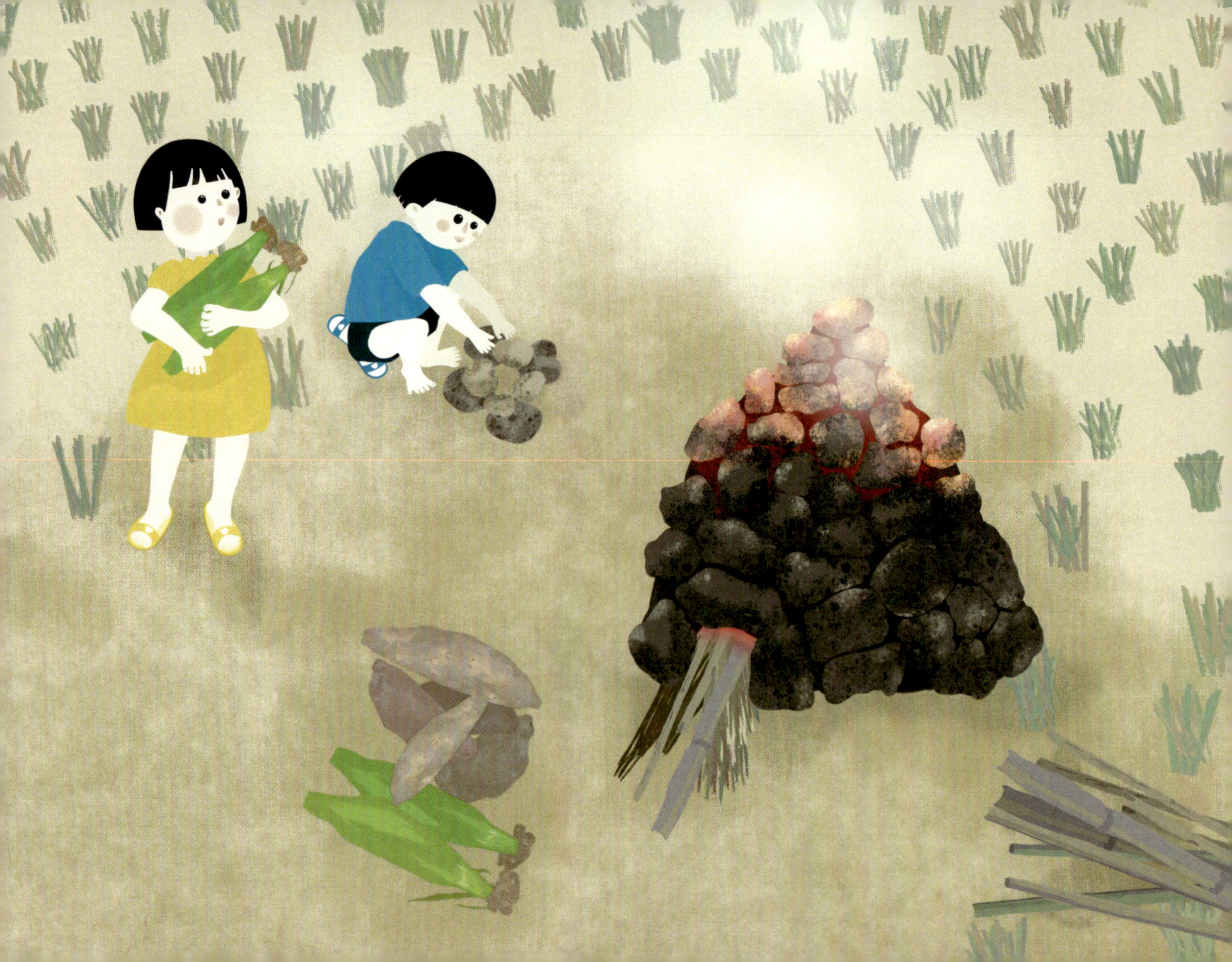

16 炕窯
Earth Oven

稻仔割了	After grain harvest,
塗焦焦	The field muds dry up.
一丸一丸若石頭	One and one resemble rocks.
一箍一箍來起窯	Round after round assemble an oven.
燃稻草	Burn the straws.
燃樹枝	Feed with woods.
塗窯紅記記	The earth oven is fired up.
炕蕃麥	Roast corn.
炕蕃薯	Roast sweet potato.
一个一个若夭鬼	One by one, all resemble gluttons.
一喙一喙食未煞	Bite by bite, none eat to fill.
細漢囡仔	While the youngest fellow
學造窯	Works on his building skill
後擺想欲炕土豆	For the next roast of peanuts.

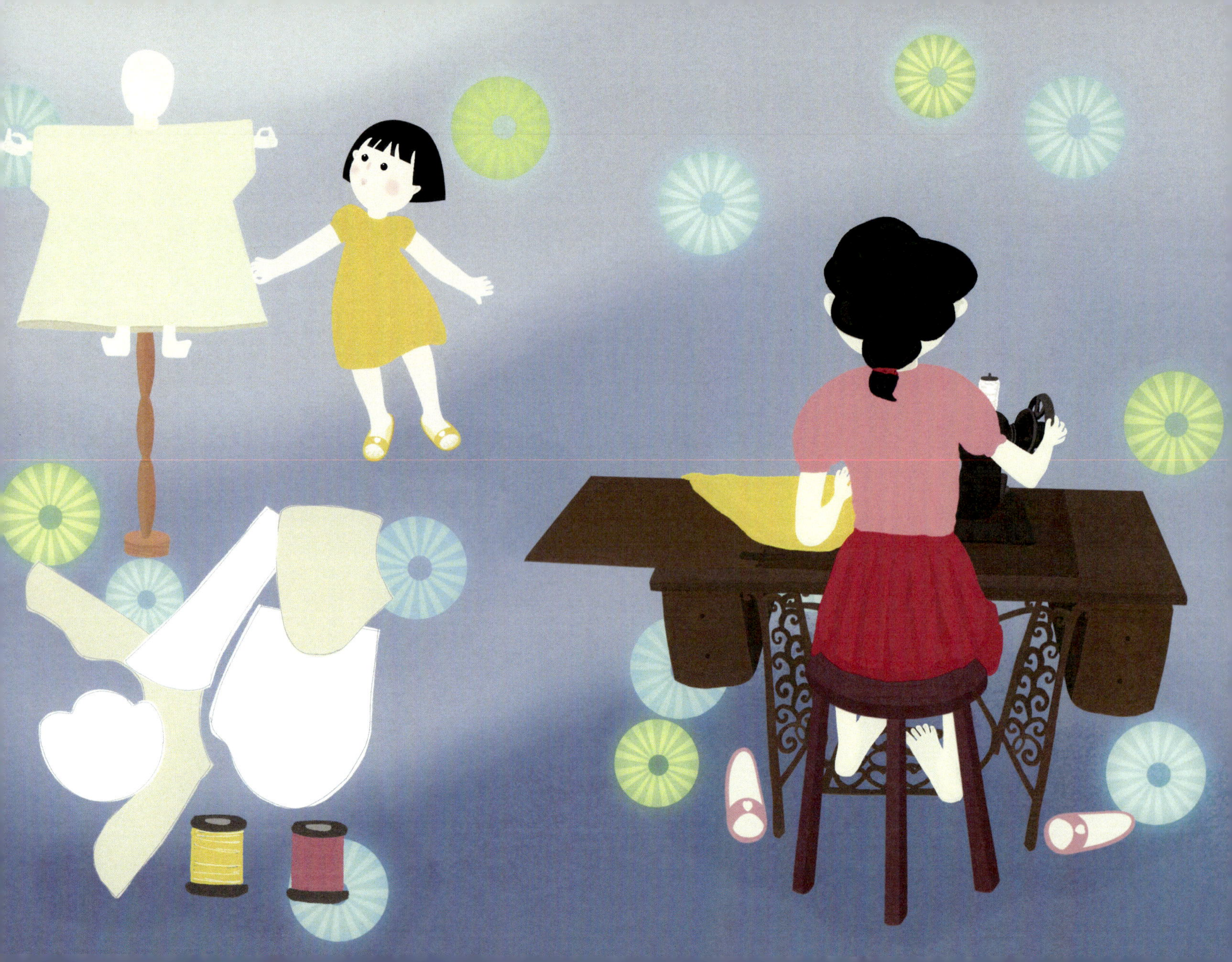

17 尪仔衫
Puppet Suits

裁縫車	The sewing machine
愛做衫	Loves to make suits,
細領的尪仔衫	Small size for glove puppets.
先鉸紙	Cut the paper pattern,
續來剪布	Then shear the cloth clean.
粉紅紗仔裙予小旦	The heroine selects a pink tulle skirt.
文生的官服著繡金線	And for the robe, put golden girt.
車啊車	Sewing and sewing,
裁縫線直直行	The thread goes straight.
一領一領新衫	Piece by piece,
跳上戲臺	New suits jump upon the stage,
也扮仙也拚性命	Playing gods and vagabonds.
金光閃閃	Glittering with strands,
攏是雙手晟	All is made by the dab hands.

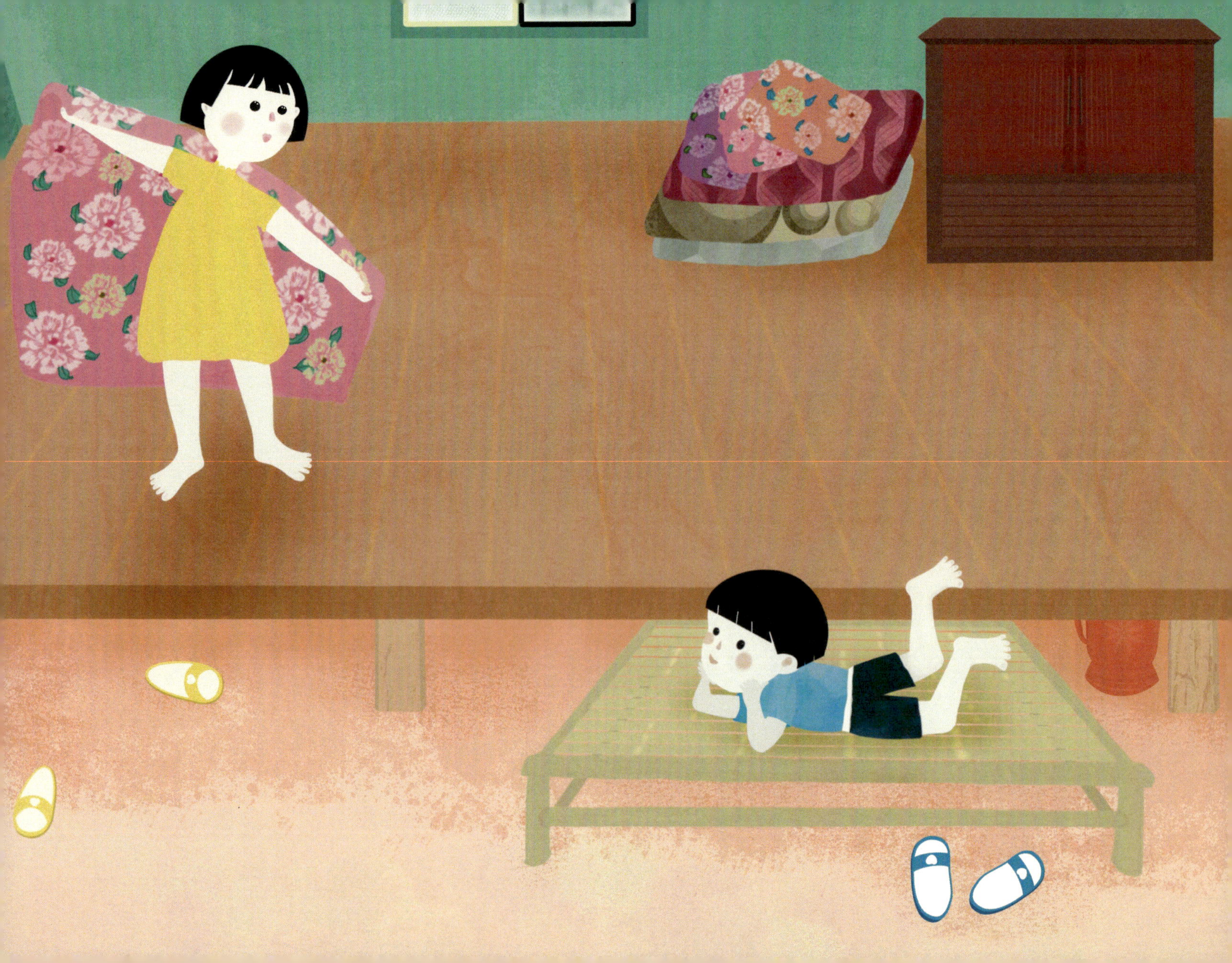

18 眠床
Bed Stage

眠床做戲臺	Bed as stage,
被單幔起來	Sheet as costume,
七字仔	Seven words give the page.
緊唸催馬	Quick chant spurs a horse.
慢調玲瓏踅	Adagio hums a wander.
一下晡	The evening entire
毋免睏晝歇嘴鼓	Acts a play without tire.
電視無愛看	The television sits unmoved
盒仔內底逐日搬	Owing to its busy schedule.
觀眾擠滿滿	Audiences crowd in the room.
哪會一个囡仔	Except a little groom,
目睭定定	Eyes fixed,
若睏若笑	With sleepy smile,
趴佇眠床跤	Lies on his stomach awhile.

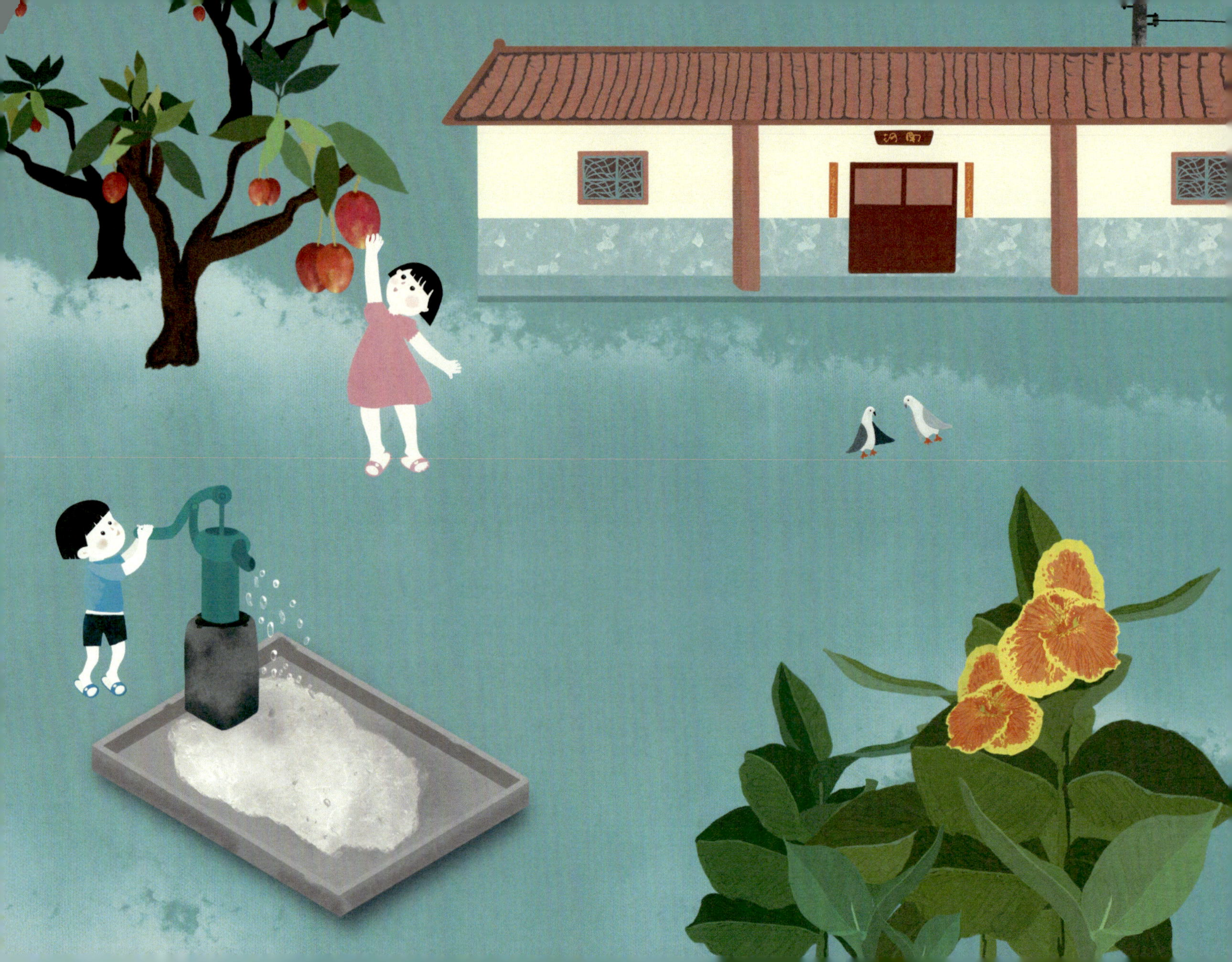

19 水搝仔
Hand Pump

這爿一口井	This nearby well
飼著千萬人	Feeds thousands grown.
彼爿一个水池	That pond afar
洇著啥物蟲	Swims bugs unknown.
一條水圳通天邊	The water way leads to heaven.
稻仔攏出穗	Rice fields all fringe
四界金鑠鑠	With golden grain tinge.
目睭也金爍爍	Your eyes also glitter
一條水路揣趣味	In seeking fun along the way.
厝邊種歡喜	All plants outdoor cheer.
蘋果檨仔紅記記	Mangos are red like apples.
鼓吹開花	Trumpet flowers twitter.
一支水搝仔	That water pump bar
恬恬等你	Waits for your revoir.

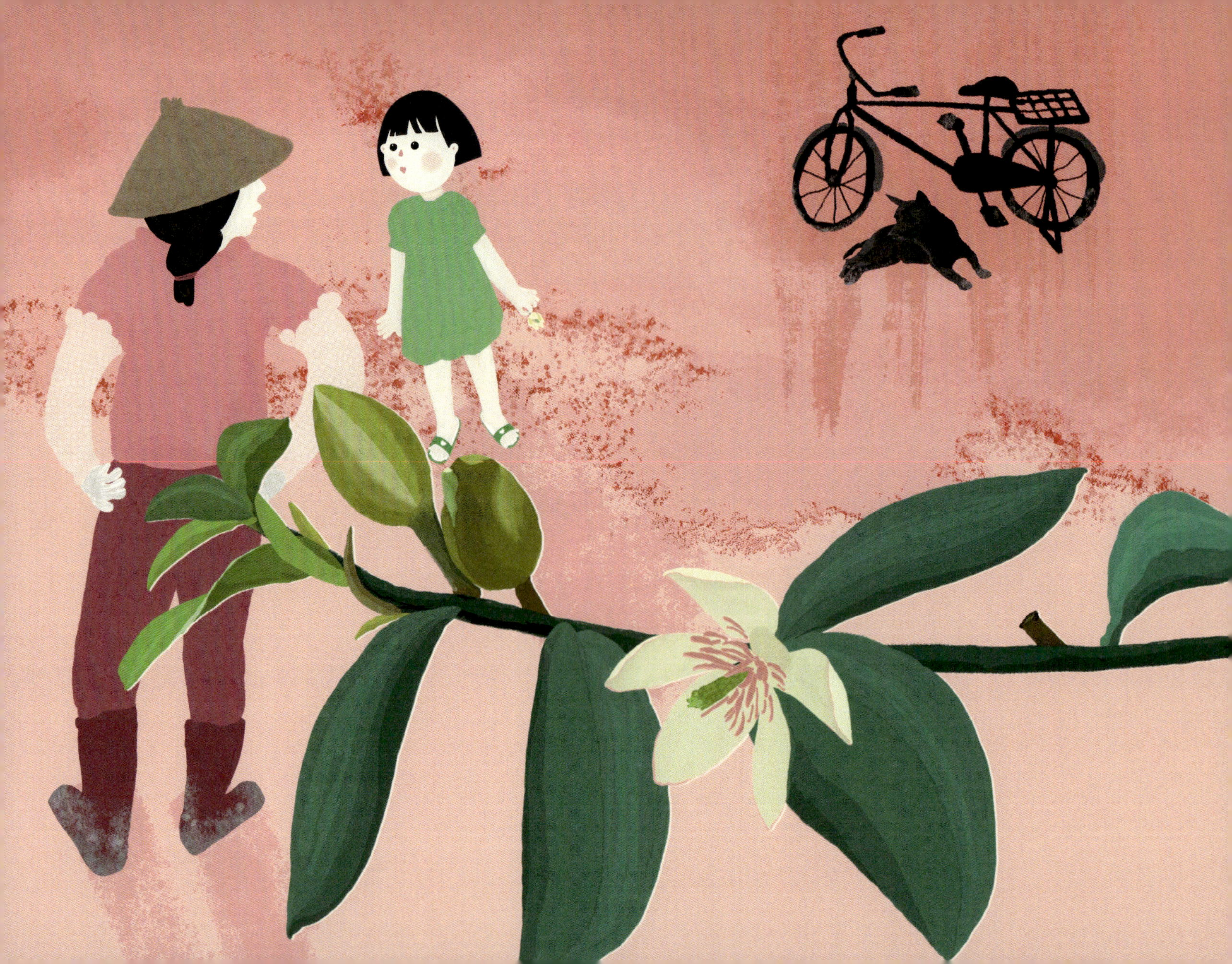

20 含笑
Beams

阿母問阮	Mom asks me
敢是汝偷挽花	Whether I pluck the flower.
阮看伊目睭降降	Her eyes devour.
煞心內著驚	My heart jumps up a tree.
雄雄越頭	Whilst turning my head,
看見	I see
睨佇彼頭的	Hiding at the corner afar,
你嘴角翹翹	Your lips curl
含笑	With beams whirl.

＊本詩獲得「送花一首詩」微詩優選，刊登於二〇〇三年五月二日《聯合報》副刊，收入二〇一三年十一月出版之《人間模樣》。

話尾
Ending Words

現此時
百款嬌
越頭走千里

Now and here
Each defines beauty
Memories go far yet clear

關於作者
About Author

蘇善

　　寫童話，寫少兒小說，更寫了不少中文詩、臺語詩與童詩，這一本雙語囡仔詩繪本的誕生，為其創作翻出了新頁。

Suzanne

　　She writes fairy tales and juvenile novels, as well as many poems in both Chinese and Taiwanese. This bilingual poetry picture book therefore marks a new chapter in her creative journey.

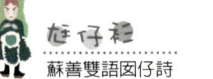

蘇善‧詩集創作
Suzanne's Poetry Collection

詩響起──蘇善詩集
定價250元

開創詩集新形式。

散文加單行詩的創新文體。

「娃系列」四輯，自2011年10月29日張貼第一則起始，在耶誕日劃下句號，兩個月的時間，共計書寫172則，約有三分之一暫未公開。

書寫猶如過篩，有些記憶被凸顯，有些必須遺忘，過程中，自我掙扎不時發生，每一次都是淬洗，煥發容顏與心境。

書寫，持續創作生命。

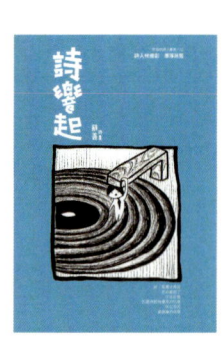

貓不捉老鼠──蘇善童話詩
定價250元

貓抓老鼠？喔不，貓兒，今天不捉老鼠！因為貓兒當學徒，做饅頭，而老鼠君，帶了一個長長的隊伍，要去給國王遞狀子，請求解除禁語令。

所以，貓鼠有事。

這事兒，關於詩。

這一本《貓不捉老鼠》包含兩個故事：〈風饅頭〉與〈東坡君與西陵君〉，都曾經發表於《國語日報》故事版，現在，這一本《貓不捉老鼠》有了讓形式與內容互相輝映的野心，並列童話與詩，瞧瞧文字可以如何一搭一唱。

詩，在童話裡面，也在童話外面。

而童話，在詩裡面，也在詩外面。

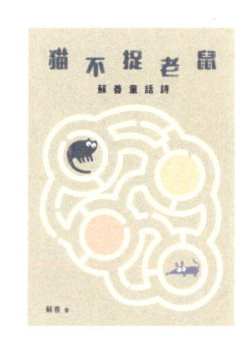

不可能平面——蘇善詩集
定價200元

寫詩，幸福，僅僅在詩裡練習胡思。

要詩不詩，干卿底事。

能詩不詩，真是枉了一路塗塗抹抹，白面之徒。

本書收錄榮獲金鼎獎以及多項文學獎的作家蘇善六十首中文詩作，皆發表於國內重要的詩刊，包括《乾坤詩刊》、《吹鼓吹詩論壇》、《野薑花雅集》以及《人間福報》副刊與《中國時報》人間副刊等。

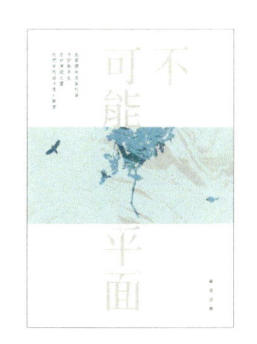

買賣——蘇善臺語詩
定價200元

本書收錄榮獲金鼎獎以及多項文學獎的作家蘇善六十首臺語詩，皆發表於國內重要臺語詩刊：《海翁台語文學》、《台文戰線》、《臺江臺語文學季刊》以及《中國時報》人間副刊等。

螞蟻路線：蘇善童詩集
定價200元

螞蟻出門上哪兒去？
工作、覓食或者嬉戲？
你瞧，詩人混進蟻群裡，
從螞蟻微小的視角感受遠大的世界，
以詩記日、記年，
以「螞蟻小語」以及「螞蟻小詩」
串聯歲時，
螞蟻來了，
邀請你，一起跟著詩人，
把語調放柔，
讓世界放遠，
想像放飛。

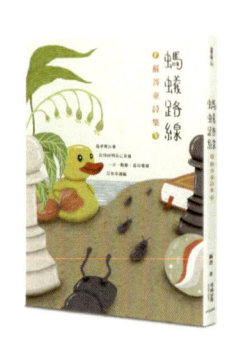

麻雀風了：蘇善童詩集
定價300元

金鼎獎作家蘇善不伏老也不牙牙學語，捧著童心，召喚松鼠、麻雀、鴿子、斑鳩、白頭翁、黑冠麻鷺、阿貓阿狗進入詩中，合演一齣齣日常驚喜！

詩集分為上下兩篇，上篇「松鼠先來報告」，松鼠蹦跳中吹起想像力的風。下篇「麻雀接著報告」，麻雀們開會、彈琴、問問題，吱吱喳喳好不熱鬧。一首詩一幅插畫，藉由充滿童趣的詩文一報告！大人視界是如何驚奇又如何美妙！

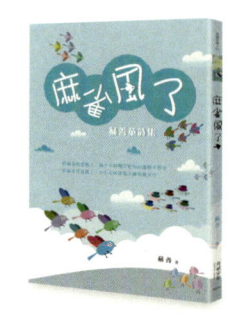

無線譜：蘇善童詩集
定價300元

時而寫詩，時而畫圖，

這一支筆吃墨二十多年，那一支筆噴彩未滿兩年，

都在一字一筆叩問，詩如何「頑」？詩如何「童」？

金鼎獎作家蘇善擁有對世間萬物的細緻洞察，並將這些感受凝鍊為充滿韻律感的文字。影子可以是巨人、夜鶯、蘋果；鳥兒、山巒也能化身成一座島……

書中每首詩作皆各自配有一幅插圖，讓讀者在文字和圖像之間來回穿梭；以童趣的角度出發，激發孩子對文學與美學的想像力及創造力。

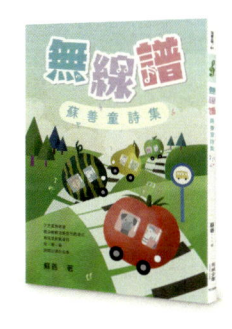

拍出花香：蘇善童詩集
定價300元

一篇詩作往往就是一張圖像印記，

一如相機的「視界」，鏡頭忽近忽遠，

時而微距時而廣角，都把觀見搜羅起來。

金鼎獎作家蘇善透過詩作及繪畫，打造充滿童趣的「視界」，她翻玩想像與詩句，將動人的瞬間以畫筆定格、收藏，陪伴孩子走過春夏秋冬。

這本詩集如同一扇窗，讓孩子們在詩與畫的世界中，發現無限的可能與夢想！

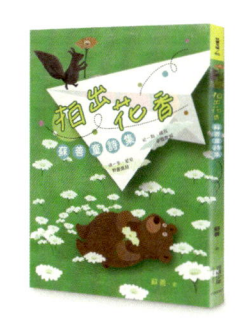

兒童文學 67　PG3160

尪仔衫 蘇善雙語囡仔詩

作者／蘇善
繪者／蘇善
責任編輯／劉芮瑜
圖文排版／陳彥妏
封面設計／嚴若綾

出版策劃／秀威少年
製作發行／秀威資訊科技股份有限公司
114 台北市內湖區瑞光路76巷65號1樓
電話：+886-2-2796-3638
傳真：+886-2-2796-1377
服務信箱：service@showwe.com.tw
http://www.showwe.com.tw

郵政劃撥／19563868
戶名：秀威資訊科技股份有限公司
展售門市／國家書店【松江門市】
104 台北市中山區松江路209號1樓
電話：+886-2-2518-0207
傳真：+886-2-2518-0778

網路訂購／秀威網路書店：https://store.showwe.tw
　　　　　　國家網路書店：https://www.govbooks.com.tw
法律顧問／毛國樑　律師

經銷／聯合發行股份有限公司
231新北市新店區寶橋路235巷6弄6號4F
電話：+886-2-2917-8022　傳真：+886-2-2915-6275

出版日期／2025年9月　BOD一版　**定價**／300元
ISBN／978-626-99790-4-2

讀者回函卡

秀威少年
SHOWWE YOUNG

版權所有・翻印必究　Printed in Taiwan　本書如有缺頁、破損或裝訂錯誤，請寄回更換
Copyright © 2025 by Showwe Information Co., Ltd.All Rights Reserved

國家圖書館出版品預行編目

尪仔衫:蘇善雙語囡仔詩 / 蘇善著. -- 一版. --
臺北市 : 秀威少年, 2025.09
  面;   公分. -- (兒童文學 ; 67)
台語、英文對照
BOD版
ISBN 978-626-99790-4-2(平裝)

863.598   114010057